HE SAID TRUST ME... HE LIED!

Deception: He Lied Miniseries

Book 4

Daphne Dennis

TLM Publishing House

Copyright

Social Stamina – 1,2,3 Let's Go!

Titles to help look at things from other perspectives and strengthen your mindset.

The Great Ascension–1,2,3 Let's Go!

Titles to help you gain focus and climb the ladder of success!

How to Start – 1,2,3 Let's Go!

Titles to help you with step-by-step, must-have knowledge of the business world and personal experiences.

Top 10 Questions to Ask Before You…1,2,3 Let's Go!

Titles with must-have questions (and logic behind) for many of life's daily and major decisions.

Find our fiction below!

https://www.ttpublishinghouse.com/legendsreborn

https://www.ttpublishinghouse.com/7wishes

https://www.ttpublishinghouse.com/mallcadet

Social Media

Facebook: tlmpublishinghouse

Website: www.TTpublishinghouse.com

Want to Read for Free?

You may qualify for a spot on our Advance Reader Copy group.

Never heard of an ARC Group?

Simply put, it's a small group of people who are interested in a specific genre and are invited to read books before they're published.

Your feedback can help alter the storyline or even catch an elusive typo!

You're asked to provide an honest review when it is published, and that's it!

You read for free!

Go now to confirm your interest in the ARC Group!
https://www.ttpublishinghouse.com/joinTLMarc

Contents

Matthew

Debbie sat in her dining room. There were light purple walls in her dining area to create a modern and welcoming atmosphere. As a result, the room had a distinct personality. It also had a mini gallery; the majority of the collection was comprised of family portraits and Vincent Van Gough's "Starry Night," which was obviously a copy. Debbie's favorite chairs ringed the table with a striped rug that sat beneath it, giving the space a personal touch.

All-day swimming, late-night cookouts, sleepovers, cars in the driveway, bikes at the ready, and beautiful mornings full of smiles were just some of the things Debbie's house was known for before the kids grew up.

Debbie jerked up at the sound of knocking coming from her front door, eyes darting around to look for a weapon before remembering the metal rat tail comb that was in her bag. She had just bought the thing in a local store near her house out of paranoia, but perhaps that was the best thing she could have done for herself. Debbie knew she could've gotten a much more traditional self-defense tool like a small knife, but then again, she also knew that she was too much of a klutz to be carrying a pocket knife everywhere. Heck, she was certain she'd probably end up hurting herself in the process of trying to defend herself with that sharp object, so a rat tail comb was far more reasonable to own. Plus, she could also use it as a comb. She felt that having something as essential as this small, supposedly harmless-looking comb was worth investing in after all the life-threatening situations she had put herself in lately. Silently, she tiptoed towards the door. A looming tense aura made her skin crawl in anxiousness as she placed her right ear on the cold wood.

Silence.

She gulped. Staring at the door with intent as one of her hands slowly crept towards the doorknob and the other, practically holding the sharp-ended comb with a death grip.

Just like we practiced. Come on. Time to put your theory to use. She psyched herself up, breathing out a quiet yet ragged breath before swinging the door open with full force, screaming at the top of her lungs in an attempt to scare away whoever was knocking earlier.

"Whoa, that's quite a scream, wouldn't you say?" A man's voice replied to her maniac screaming, followed by a soft chuckle. Debbie stood there dumbfounded as her gaze was greeted by none other than the handsome detective that somehow frequented her humble abode, smiling at her with a raised eyebrow.

"Matthew... What brings you here..." she paused to look at her watch before looking back at him with a questioning gaze, "... this late at night?"

"Ah. That. I just wanted to check up on you and see if there were any new leads you could provide. I think I did the right thing visiting you, though, since you look like you were about to do some damage with that comb in your hand." He finished, nodding his head with amusement toward the metal comb in her hand that was still suspended mid-air. Debbie quickly hid her hand behind her back, laughing nervously at him before checking outside. Nothing.

"Are you alright?"

"Huh?" She looked up, confused.

Matthew twisted his body slightly from side to side as if checking to see if there was anything behind him, confusing Debbie even more.

"What are you doing?" She asked again once the detective turned his attention back to her.

"Ah, well, you kept looking past me, so I was wondering if you were expecting someone else... Is it your husband?" He spoke, tone shifting sounding a little odd as he asked the question.

"No. It's not him. It's... No one." She faltered, immediately giving him a feigned innocent smile as she opened the door wider for him. "Come in. I'll make you some coffee."

Matthew gratefully accepted as they walked to her living room. It still looked the same, mostly, except for the new blackout lilac-colored curtains and some evidently new pepper spray devices lined up on her coffee table. There were about 5 of them, he noted with great curiosity as he sat on the couch.

"With creamer?" Debbie shouted from the kitchen.

"A little, please." He shouted back.

Debbie later came back holding a tray that contained two cups, one coffee and one hot cocoa, with some jam biscuits and butter cookies, setting the tray down at the coffee table before she herself sat next to the waiting detective.

"So, how have you been lately?" He broke the ice first.

"Oh, you know, the usual." She answered, chuckling half-heartedly before sighing and pursing her lips. "Honestly? I've been on edge lately."

"Why's that?"

"It happened after Herman died," she hesitated, her fingers fidgeting and drawn together as she stared at the floor. "I... I thought I was just being paranoid and all because my friend and her previous boss died, and I didn't see it coming. I felt like someone was stalking me, but I decided to shrug it off. Still, I had proven myself wrong that it wasn't just paranoia."

Matthew reached for his coffee, "What makes you say that? Did you see someone?"

"I've seen a man. He wears a suit and has been following me around these past few weeks. Gosh, perhaps even longer than that."

"Do you know what he's after?" Matthew questioned again.

Debbie shook her head, genuinely puzzled and distraught. "I don't know, maybe because I'm following the case. Maybe because I coincidentally saw the bodies first. Maybe because they're planning to take me next."

"Hey, Debbie. It's okay. You're safe with me now. Calm down." Matthew's words rung in her ears as she felt one of his hands rest on hers, effectively halting the rocking of her legs that she was unconsciously doing out of fear. She looked up at him, letting a sigh of gratitude escape while smiling softly at Matthew.

"Thanks," she muttered, inhaling and exhaling deeply to gather herself and continue talking about her findings. However, it wasn't as easy as before, not solely because she found it hard to relive the memories without trembling but because of Matthew's warm hand on hers. She didn't think that the man would show this much sympathy, but she wasn't complaining.

Debbie furrowed her eyebrows to concentrate on her story and away from the lingering thoughts of the heat of his hand on hers and how handsome he was.

Okay, whoa, going off the rails again there. Not good, Debbie. Not good.

"You were spacing out while staring intently at my hand. Are you… uncomfortable?"

"Oh no, no. It's not that. Not at all!" She flustered, her cheeks turning red. It might seem silly, but she felt like one of those main characters in those romantic books she loved to read during her youth.

"Ah. That's good then." Matthew offered a light smile. "Anymore to tell?"

"I also met with Ed."

That caught the detective's full attention because she could quite literally feel him grip her hand at the sudden mention of his name, for God knows what reason. Debbie's wincing expression snapped him out of his unconscious grip, apologizing while simultaneously pulling his hand away like he was burned by a blazing fire.

"Sorry. I didn't mean to grip your hand. Did I hurt you?" He asked, completely trying to steer the situation to his advantage. Unfortunately for him, Debbie was quite the curious cat.

"Not really, no. I'm fine. Why did you do that, anyway? Do you hate my husband?" That last bit rolled out so easily from her tongue that she herself held her breath. It wasn't that she stopped calling Ed her husband in front of other people, but the way it slipped out of her lips sounded as if she was defending Ed against any prejudice Matthew might have against him.

"I just don't think you should trust people so easily, Debbie. Not even your husband."

Debbie couldn't help but laugh sadly at that. "Well, you're right about that. We have met a few times already. I've tried figuring out what was going on in that head of his every time we met. He told me he was trying to solve the case himself, which to me sounded ludicrous because he didn't know Judy very well. I don't think I ever noticed or heard of them spending time together."

"Why does he want to solve the case? Did he ever tell you?"

"Yes. He said he wanted to give me some peace of mind, but I told him I knew he was lying."

The detective nodded at her, evidently deep in thought, before proceeding to give Debbie a consoling pat on her upper arm just below her shoulder.

"It must be so hard, hearing lies from someone you care about. If I were him, I'd never lie to you. You deserve trust... and love. You deserve the best." He stated, thumb gently caressing her upper arm as he locked eyes with her as if he was seeing her soul. Debbie's inner thoughts were in disarray when he started leaning closer, those mysteriously enchanting eyes making her freeze. It made her feel fragile, so seen, so *bare*. And somehow, just when she thought she would feel secure, she felt afraid, too afraid to be this bare in front of someone else with no facade, mask off whatever it was she was thinking and feeling.

"I… I think I need to rest. You should get going too. It's rather late." She whispered as she lightly backed away and turned her face away from his, which was about an inch from hers. Matthew didn't reply to that, only moving away and sighing quietly. They walked towards the front door, neither of them knowing what to say after that awkward moment in which they almost kissed, but Debbie didn't enjoy having this strange, awkward air around her and Matthew, so she blurted out whatever her brain could manage.

"Oh. Yes. Remember Bobo? He talked about weird things. And by weird, I mean *weird* weird. Like having a mouse friend or whatever and people in trees." She shivered at the thought of the eccentric man as she remembered her first encounter with him. "Anyway, I thought he was just like any other ordinary crazed homeless man at first, but he told me something unsettling. He saw a man with a gun the night of Judy's murder. The man was asking for the papers."

Matthew's face might have been stoic, but a flicker of something ignited in his eyes.

"I see. The papers. If you have any idea or if you've seen them, tell me immediately."

Debbie nodded at that. They exchanged goodbyes, and, just as the detective was taking his leave, he halted, turning back to her with a serious look.

"I almost forgot to tell you something important and the real purpose of my visit."

"What is it?"

"You need to pay Philip as well."

Debbie clenched the doorknob and froze momentarily.

How in the world did Matthew know about Philip? She never told him. Was he also following the same lead as her?

"H-huh? What's that drug dealer got to do with it?"

Matthew shook his head. "Philip is not a drug dealer. He's a spy."

Ed

"Are you sure you're going out now? You just got better, Debbie." Patty asked in concern as she watched Debbie get dressed to go out. Patty had gotten a sudden message from her an hour ago saying she was feeling better and that Fluffy could return home so she immediately packed the fluffy dog's stuff and drove to Debbie's without hesitation, although she didn't understand how Debbie could go out just after having been sick. If it were up to Patty, she would want her friend to stay a day or two more to fully recover. And Debbie would've listened to her and rested more.

That was, of course, if Debbie was sick at all.

"I'll be fine, Patty. I've recovered. Thank you for lending me your car as well. I don't think my car has gas right now, so I really needed yours."

"That's alright. Just make sure to bring it back in one piece. And you too, of course." Patty joked as they chuckled.

"Thank you for taking care of Fluffy for me as well while I was sick, and thank you for agreeing to dogsit today. I promise I'll make it up to you somehow." She smiled while her friend just playfully rolled her eyes back at her.

"Oh, come on. You make it sound like it's a difficult task to look after Mr. Fluffy. He's such a gentleman!" Patty squealed as she hugged the unsuspecting dog who walked in front of her. Debbie giggled at the scene, finding it childlike yet adorable.

"I better be on the road now." She said after looking at her wristwatch, hooking the long strap of her canvas bag over her shoulder, and giving Fluffy a kiss on the forehead before finally hugging her friend.

"Please be careful when you're driving."

"I will. Oh, and I'll appreciate it if you don't open the curtains at all. The sun makes the inside of the house a lot warmer than I prefer." She lied, but Patty bought it anyway.

Debbie bolted to her friend's car, started the engine, and drove off. She kept looking at the mirrors to see if someone was following her. Thankfully, her plan worked. She was on her way to Ed's motel room when she saw from a distance two men fighting near the motel. Squinting, she soon realized it was her husband having a fistfight with a man in a suit.

"Shoot." She cursed, worried for Ed as she tried to drive faster. As if struck by bad luck, a red-light signal turned on as people carried on with their lives as if someone wasn't being attacked just a short distance away from them. How much of an unconcerned world this had become. Debbie almost yelled at them to move so she could help her husband.

They continued fighting. Ed fell to the ground twice, but he quickly gained the upper hand as they wrestled on the pavement of the motel's parking lot. Though, it ended sooner than expected as the other gave him a solid punch on the stomach, causing Ed to cough out some blood and curl into a ball. Debbie knew that if she didn't act quickly, her husband would be no more.

Then the signal changed.

Green light. Gas pedal down. Horn blaring.

"Get away from my husband, you jerk!" She shouted, scaring the man with a suit away as she acted like she was going to run over him. That was probably his instinct, telling him the right thing since Debbie, in fact, wanted to run him over at that very moment.

The man limped to his car hurriedly before fleeing the scene leaving poor, beaten, and bloodied Ed on the pavement squirming and moaning in pain. Debbie rushed to his side, trembling slightly and panicking as she tried to think of the best option.

"I should call the hospital. And Matth-" She was cut off from speaking just as a hand grasped her frantic hands that were searching for her phone in her pockets. She looked at him, muddled and worried-sick, with knitted eyebrows and a big frown, but Ed only tightened his hold. It wasn't painful, but it was enough to get the point across. Debbie grimaced but nonetheless helped him stand on his feet.

She practically dragged him, which was no easy feat, toward his motel room, which looked even messier than it had been before.

"Are you hoarding trash or what? Look at this man cave you've got going on." She huffed, letting Ed plop to his already dirtied bed with a soft thud.

Ed groaned, still in pain. "Never mind the mess. Just get out of here quickly before that man returns with back-up."

"And leave you here in this miserable state? Look, Ed, I know we're not fully there yet with whatever you want to call our relationship, but I still care about you." Debbie pointed out, exasperated at the fact that Ed kept on pushing her away when all she ever wanted was to understand him.

"All the more reason I need you to stay as far away as possible from this case, Debbie."

Debbie scoffed, rolling her eyes in irritation while still looking for anything remotely close to a first aid kit? Really? How had the man survived this long without one? She then found a clean cloth, the cleanest of the bunch that was messily shoved inside a drawer, before hurrying to the bathroom to gather lukewarm water and some soap. At the very least, Debbie knew how to clean wounds, thanks to her own clumsiness.

"Ouch! Gosh, are you trying to kill me?" Ed winced as Debbie patted the slightly damped cloth on his face. That only caused the woman to intentionally press a bit harsher with her frown deepening.

Debbie said, "Suck it up. Do you have any arnica lying around here somewhere?"

Ed looked at her for a moment before sighing and cocking his head towards one of the smaller drawers. "Top left, third row. I keep my medicines and things there."

She followed his direction, and sure enough, there was an arnica gel inside the drawer alongside a white powdery substance inside a tiny zip lock baggie.

"Debbie?" Ed called out after the woman went silent. "Did you find the gel?"

"I did..." she replied, turning to him with disbelief as she held the tiny zip lock for him to see. "I also found this, Ed."

Debbie observed the way Ed's swollen eyes grew nervous, fearful, and a little sad. Was that because she found something she shouldn't have?

Is this why he couldn't tell me anything?

Ed said, "Debbie, please, it's not-"

"It's not what, Ed? Not narcotics?" She finished. Clear rage and betrayal flashed on her face and eyes. "Is this why you're so hellbent on solving this case? Because you're afraid that whatever or whoever was killing those that use narcotics would end up killing you too? Is that why you own a gun without ever telling me?"

"Debbie, just drop the-"

"NO!" Debbie shouted, angry tears rolling down her eyes as she threw the little sachet at him. "Do I have to find things out all by myself? Does it entertain you seeing me go into this stupid game like I'm treasure hunting for your secrets when I'm your wife?! What's the next secret that I'll uncover, huh? Tell me, Ed. That you owe money to those men, and that's why they're trying to beat you to death?"

"It's baking soda," Ed replied.

"Really? So, why won't you tell me what's going on?!"

"BECAUSE I WANT TO KEEP YOU SAFE!" Ed finally snapped back, face pained and filled with guilt. "I'm doing this because I want you to be able to still live a normal life, Debbie. That's why I'm begging you to drop the case. I've been begging you from the start because I care, too. I don't want anything bad to happen to you. I don't care what happens to me; they could beat me to death, but I can't stand the idea of getting you into this mess, and that's the reason why I don't tell you anything."

The room went silent after that, just the two of them looking at each other, trying to figure out what to do with their ever-messy relationship.

"I wish you could've said that from the start, Ed." Debbie started off. She no longer felt rage but a deep sense of regret and disappointment over their misunderstandings. "I wish you could just tell me what's going on so I can trust you. But we're both too deep in this mess to even try to walk away. We both have our feet on the grave by now, and you know that."

"I'm sorry. I should have given you at least a short explanation rather than nothing at all."

"Even if you did, I don't think I would've just stood idly by after Judy's death. In the end, I would still put my life on the line to find the truth."

Ed let out a small, sad chuckle. "You've always been that kind of girl."

Debbie smiled sadly before sighing. "I'll leave for now. Patty is in the house, so I'm still wary that she'll meet one of those men by accident. Make sure to put arnica on your bruises to lessen the swelling, and please, stay inside your room in the meantime. Secure the lock if you must."

Ed nodded, unable to look her in the eye. Debbie was already at his front door when Ed called out to her again.

"Debbie."

"What is it, Ed?"

He had hesitation in his eyes while gazing back at her, as he always did. "I… T… Take care on your way back home."

Debbie felt her heart sink to the floor, yet she looked emotionless.

"… I will."

Philip

The drive home was longer than expected. She went to get some strong wine in hopes that maybe that would help get things off her mind. She even thought of asking Patty to sleep over and share the drink with her. She needed any distraction she could find to stray from the breaking of her heart.

"Patty, I'm back. Fluffy?" She called out after opening the front door, dropping her keys off at the entrance table with a clinking sound. Usually, that would alert her dog and send him running down the hallway, but not this time.

He must be so busy playing with Patty that he doesn't hear me now. She reasoned as she called for the two again.

And again, nothing. Nothing seemed out of the ordinary; the blinds were still closed, the yard was clean, and the hallway was spotless.

No. It shouldn't be this quiet. Not with Patty or Fluffy, who would definitely greet her by the door.

She walked closer to the living room, heart thumping out of her chest and drumming in her eardrums as she gulped in fear. Debbie was stunned and frozen like a statue, standing by the entrance of her living room as Patty lay on the floor, unmoving, with a broken cup next to her. On the couch sat a man in a suit who was sipping a cup of coffee that looked identical to the one next to her unconscious friend.

"So, you're back." The man stated, setting the cup of coffee down.

"What are you doing here? How did you get in?"

"One question at a time, Debbie," the man replied. "I got here because that lovely lady allowed me to enter."

"What did you do to her? Where's my dog?" She was afraid, palms damp with sweat, and her knees felt like they would give out at any moment.

"Your dog is safe in your room, and she's not dead. Don't worry. She doesn't have any valuable assets to be targeted anyway besides being friends with you. She's simply...*napping*."

"Quit playing games, Philip, and tell what you're after. If it's the papers, then I'm sorry, but I don't have them."

"You know, it was too easy to track you down. You leave traces everywhere. You ask innocent people to help you and put them in a place you know is dangerous." Philip leaned on the couch to look back at her comfortably. It was sickening how at ease he was while she was trembling in horror inside her own home.

"I don't have the papers. I don't even know what they are."

"Then tell me more about poor lovely Judy. Did she ever tell you anything strange? Give you eccentric gifts or-"

"She gave me nothing. I asked for nothing. Please stop bothering me before I call the police."

Philip only raised an eyebrow at her, slightly amused that the woman gathered so much courage as to pull her phone out and showed it to him, albeit her trembling didn't go unnoticed.

Philip said, "Ah, the usual threat. I'll have you know that I have a perfect alibi for the night of the murder. There's just no way I could have been there." He paused, gasping with feigned innocence as his eyes widened. "But you don't, right? You don't have a good alibi as to why you were the first person to see the bodies. Two bodies, to be exact."

"I'm working with the police and the chief detective on the case. They'll believe me over you."

"Do you really think those foolish dogs could ever be on par with me?" Debbie's fear grew tenfold as the man laughed maniacally as if he was losing his wits. "My God, Debbie. Oh, naïve Debbie. They stand no chance against me. I rule over people, one word, and whoever I wish to be eliminated will be off the radar in no time. Say a word about me, and you might as well start sleeping with both eyes open."

Philip stood up, making Debbie flinch and let go of the phone. He continued walking while she stepped back until she was up against the wall. She was so terrified that she dropped to her knees, shaking, lips opening and closing like a fish out of water. Philip crouched down to level their eyesight, his mood drastically changing into a deadlier one as he grabbed Debbie's face with one hand, blunt nails digging into her cheeks as tears started rolling down her face. That was the first time she really felt like she was going to die.

She never thought she'd regret contacting the man until that very moment as he leaned closer to her ear, turning her face forcefully to the side as she whimpered.

"A friendly tip from me to you, my dear," Philip muttered, voice low and menacing. "Never play games with me. I always win."

"Let go of her, you son of a bitch!" Debbie felt like air suddenly flowed through her body again as the hand from her face pulled away. Philip dodged an attack and stood up, hands in his pockets, as he gave the other man a fake smile.

"My, my. Here comes your knight in shining armor to the rescue. I was never informed that you two still live together. Perhaps I miscalculated some things."

He mused, watching as the man helped Debbie by shielding her from him.

To say that Debbie was surprised would be a great understatement; she was, in all honestly, bewildered beyond belief that her husband would show up instead of Matthew.

Debbie whispered, "Why are you here?"

"I followed you home because I felt like something bad was going to happen."

"Aw, look at you both. Acting so sweet... How disgusting."

"You're disgusting. Entering my wife's house and threatening her. What kind of coward are you?!" Ed spat, and that seemed to hit a nerve. However, the clouds that were brooding over his eyes cleared as he adjusted his suit.

Philip said, "I'm simply paying a visit to see if you've found the papers. Isn't that your real purpose as well, Ed?"

"Leave," Ed commanded while Philip chuckled softly.

Philip said, "Stand down, dog. I already got what I came for."

Philip turned his attention to Debbie, who quickly hid behind Ed.

"I'll see you around, Debbie. Be careful."

With that, he left without another word. Debbie's body shut down on her as she slid further to the floor with a shaky sigh, eyes wavering as if she had seen her nightmare come to life. Ed sighed, helping her to the couch, but not before cursing in surprise at the sight of Patty lying on the floor.

"She's fine. I think Philip spiked her drink, but she's safe… mostly." Debbie explained, though still a little shaken up herself when she saw her husband's confused expression.

"You let just anyone in your house?" Ed asked, unamused. Debbie could only sigh, as she had no energy to argue after everything that had happened earlier. "She's not just anyone, Ed. She's my friend."

"A friend that lets strangers in."

"It's not her fault. I didn't think Philip would track me down."

"See?! *This*," he said with a displeased frown. "This is why I don't want you getting involved with this mess. You are *too* trusting. You can't let anyone in your house. Not even the closest of your friends. How did you even meet that bastard?"

"I met him a while ago."

"And you didn't bother telling me?" Ed asked, completely offended. Debbie pinched the bridge of her nose. This wasn't exactly the right time to argue over every detail. And how dare he sound so offended when he's hiding so many more secrets.

"I have my secrets too, Ed. Just like you have yours." She rebutted, catching him off guard as he cleared his throat in frustration.

Ed said, "Anyway, I don't want you meeting that man ever again. He's dangerous."

"How did you know that?"

"Because I saw how he threatened you. He's clearly someone of influence." Debbie deserved that. "And because I've been following the case and came to a similar conclusion as you did. Look, I know him because I borrowed some money from him once."

Debbie blinked at him. "You what? Why?"

"That doesn't matter now, but the point is I know he's not good news and might be the murderer, so you shouldn't meet him for any reason. You could end up dead like Judy did, and I… I don't want that to happen, not to you. I want to protect you, Debbie. I've always wanted to protect you."

She was flustered by his sudden concern, unable to rebut until it sunk in that, even though it was a nice gesture, it couldn't erase 25 years of doing what he said, always listening to him and following his orders like a marionette on strings. She never felt like she was allowed to have an opinion. It was tiring to handle all of that, on top of his unwillingness, to be honest. She was sick of his male dominance and authoritative demeanor even when they no longer lived in the same house, no longer even acting as husband and wife.

"I know what to do, Ed. I may be a klutz, but I'm not an idiot. Go, I'll handle Patty myself."

Ed couldn't find any reason to stay as he saw how serious she was about having him leave. So, with a long sigh, he left, locking the door in case Debbie forgot. Debbie ran a hand through her hair, still overwhelmed with the events that had conspired in the span of a day. She heaved as she dragged Patty to the couch; thankfully, she was breathing steadily. Debbie even checked for any bruises, but thankfully there were none. Going to her room, she saw Fluffy sleeping on the floor, probably given the same medication as Patty.

I need to solve this case before things escalate further. She thought to herself as she brushed Fluffy's fur.

"I'm sorry, Fluffy. You got involved in this mess because of me." She whispered, giving the sleeping dog a kiss on the head. She washed up, no longer having an appetite to eat nor interest in the wine that was long forgotten at the entrance hallway. She fell to her bed like a log. The last thing she could remember thinking of was how she was more desperate than ever to figure the case out herself. Judy was her friend, not Ed's, so no one could blame her for suspecting that her husband was still lying to her.

It was tiring, everything was, and so, with little resistance, she let herself succumb to exhaustion.

Date Night

The next day, Debbie apologized profusely to Patty for endangering her life. Though Patty said it was nothing, she could tell from the look on her face that she was terrified. Debbie would be too. Patty had never experienced half of what she had gone through since Judy's death.

Debbie resumed going to work, although she still felt wary of her surroundings; the bills wouldn't pay themselves just because her life was in danger. Although that was sad, it was her reality. Her routine was waking up at least 30 minutes early, getting ready, circling around town for good measure to make sure that no one was following her before going to work, working but still being vigilant, taking breaks where no one could find her or see her, beginning shifts again, circling around town and going back home. Thankfully, she encountered none of those strange men in suits.

Were they tired of following me around, or were they able to gain access to whatever it was that they needed?

In some sense, that felt impossible.

Slowly, it was becoming more mundane, so eerily mundane that she guarded herself more. There were no longer surprises, no life-threatening situations, and it felt odd. She was no longer used to living the ordinary life she had led before the case. She could no longer enjoy simple things like going shopping without having to look around in case someone was following her. To her surprise, however, Matthew came up to her after her shift that Friday to ask her formally for a date Saturday night. It came out of nowhere, but the man said he had been interested to know more about her ever since they met. Of course, Debbie agreed; it wasn't every day that a handsome detective asked her on a date.

She got excited, briefly forgetting that her life had become mundane in the middle of almost finishing the case. She looked through her wardrobe for any plausible outfit only to settle on a grey classy yet casual long-sleeved wrap-pleated maxi dress and some white sneakers. Matthew never disclosed the name of the place they would have their date, so she thought playing it safe with a casual dress would be the best idea. Saturday evening came faster than she had expected as she soon found herself staring at the dashing detective who was already standing in front of her door, a bouquet of red roses in hand. He was handsome, wearing a plain black long-sleeved polo shirt that was rolled up to his elbows, showing off the golden Rolex wrapped around his wrist. He paired it with black trousers and some polished formal shoes with his hair styled with gel. *God, he's so hot.*

"Wow, you look amazing." He mused, offering the flower to her with a smile as she blushed.

"Thank you; you don't look so shabby yourself." She replied with a shy laugh, to which he chuckled.

"Well, I try not to be. Ready to go, then?"

Debbie nodded, thanking Matthew as he assisted her to his car. They drove to a 5-star restaurant in a neighboring town, the detective explaining that he frequently had to travel from town to town while solving cases and found the place by accident. It was classy with marbled floor and walls, and its golden touches screamed high-end.

"Are you sure you want to eat here? I don't mind eating at a local diner." Debbie whispered as they walked towards the reservation desk.

"Please, what kind of man would I be to have you settle for anything less than the best?" He chuckled before greeting the man holding the reservation book. "Reservation under the name Matthew, table 14."

"Ah, the usual, sir. Of course." The man nodded with a polite smile before having someone usher them to their table.

The usual? Debbie thought.

"Do you bring girls here to date periodically?" She questioned. Matthew raised both eyebrows at her before breaking into a soft fit of laughter.

"Not at all. You're the first woman I have ever brought here. Why do you ask?"

Debbie suddenly felt ashamed for asking but at the same time proud that she was the first to have this kind of date with Matthew. "Well, the guy at the reservation desk said 'the usual,' so I thought... you know."

"Ah, that's because I come here alone to have their Ravioli Di Erbette from time to time. I just fell in love with the flavor of the pasta, and so I wanted to share that love with you."

Debbie blushed even more when he smiled at her, glancing away in fear that she might faint if she kept staring at him. Lucky for her, the lady that ushered them to their table announced that they had arrived. However, Debbie was confused to see a double door instead of a table.

"What's this?" She couldn't help but ask, but Matthew only chuckled before pushing one door open for her.

Good heavens, it's otherworldly beautiful.

"Oh my gosh, Matthew... This is... *Wow.*" She was at a loss for words. Their table wasn't just any table; it had a beige tent with oak wood, and, the foundations of the tent were cemented on a sofa-like ceramic with soft pillows and fluffy seat cushions. The table was big enough for two to dine, made of the same ceramic and wood base. The tent also had curtains you could pull for some privacy and a lovely little chandelier in the middle.

The tent was surrounded by trees making it cooler and fresher than most spots inside the dining hall.

Just how rich is Matthew? Debbie wondered.

"Do you like it? This is the best view they have here."

"Like it? Please, I am in love. I get why you always come back to this place. It's gorgeous." She replied as they both took seats opposite each other.

"A gorgeous place for the most gorgeous woman in this entire restaurant." He teased while Debbie playfully rolled her eyes at his compliment.

Debbie said, "You must be such a Casanova. You know how to flirt your way into a woman's heart."

Matthew replied with a sly smirk, teasing her further. "I beg to differ. I only say what I see."

"Then you must really have bad eyesight." She laughed but was surprised when Matthew took both her hands.

Looking straight at her with a serious look, he spoke. "I mean it. You are beautiful, so please don't sell yourself short because you deserve better than that."

The food came, and they enjoyed their meal while chatting and laughing. Soon, they finished the entire course and were simply enjoying the view when Matthew broke the peaceful silence.

"I like you, Debbie."

Debbie turned to look at him, contemplating, searching, and assessing. "What do you like about me?"

"You're beautiful, and you have such a wonderful personality. What is there not to like about you?"

She looked away, a sad smile creeping onto her face. "If that's the case, then why did Ed still choose to leave and lie?"

They locked eyes, staring into each other's souls as the detective muttered under his breath.

"Trust me, Debbie. I would never hurt you the way your husband does. You are worth more than that. You are worth much more than what you get from him."

Debbie didn't flinch this time when Matthew leaned in, putting his soft lips, which tasted like strawberries, on hers. Nothing much happened after that, as the detective brought her back home almost past midnight. They muttered small *"Thank yous"* and *"Goodbyes"* before Matthew drove off. That night was one of the first times she'd gotten sleep since her friend's death.

Unfortunately, her little bubble of fantasy would soon be disrupted when she accidentally drew her curtains that Sunday morning. She had gotten so complacent that the weird stalker had shown up again; there he was, on that forsaken spot where he had parked his car like always. She felt chills run up her spine as the man seemed to notice that she was looking through her living room window, almost ripping the curtains down, trying to close them.

"No... No... Why is he back again?" She breathed out, on the verge of having a panic attack as her throat closed up and her eyes watered in sheer terror. She staggered back before running to the second floor and almost knocking over Fluffy. Debbie stumbled along with Fluffy's surprised whimper as he immediately escaped to her room; she followed him to apologize.

"I'm sorry. I'm sorry. I didn't mean to kick you." She stammered. "Gosh. What should I do, Fluffy? I thought that man had gotten tired of me, but he returned. What should I do? I'm so scared."

The man had never changed spots and hadn't come closer than where he parked, but the sole thought of having someone monitoring her every move caused her so much anxiety, especially after Philip's threat and Ed almost getting kidnapped. She wanted the case to be over and to have her regular life back. It was very weird for her that anyone would be willing to keep tabs on her unless maybe she had hit a nerve. She hadn't, not until Philip, perhaps.

But the stalking started way before her encounter with Philip in her house. The man didn't seem like the type who would hold grudges over spilled ice cream. The only thing she could think of was that she'd been friends with Judy, and Judy had been affiliated with him.

"The papers. It must be because of those damn papers." She told Fluffy before perking up.

Papers... Then that must mean something is written on them... right? Something important... But...

Debbie scrambled to her feet to check her laptop. She sat on her bed, tapping her thigh impatiently as the screen loaded.

"What if... the papers weren't literally papers at all..." she whispered to herself, as her mind skipped around at the speed of light. She typed and clicked on the email icon. She went through email after email before stopping at one that was over a month old.

Clicking on it, it showed a digital card Judy had sent her for her birthday over a month ago. If you look at it, the card screamed 'made by Judy' with letters, numbers, and emojis. Debbie never really thought much of it, thinking that Judy was just being Judy, but now that she looked at it again, the card was a little odd.

"There must be a cryptic message on it. I'm sure of it now. But what is it? Goodness, Judy, why are you making my brain hurt with your riddles?" She sighed in frustration. Either this letter could lead her to Judy's killer or the reason for her death, or she could be overanalyzing things.

"No." Even though she still didn't have a concrete clue who could have possibly killed Judy, she knew that this letter might mean something. "Don't you think so too?" She asked Fluffy, who began scratching his collar intensely while whimpering. Debbie found that peculiar. Fluffy never scratched his collar that much, nor did he ever whimper as if something was scratching his neck.

"Fluffy, come here." She commanded, putting aside her laptop as her dog obliged.

"Up. Come on. Let me see what's itchy." She added, patting her thigh to make her dog stand up. Fluffy did as he was told and even raised his head for her to see. Debbie scanned underneath the collar in case there were some mites but found nothing.

Then she saw a tiny dot of blinking red and noticed that the collar was not the same collar he had before. Debbie had been on this case long enough to know what that blinking red was.

A listening device. How did Fluffy get that? Her mind echoed.

"There's nothing there. I think you just need a bath in case there are mites." She said nonchalantly, hoping that whoever was listening to her wouldn't notice that she had found out. Debbie unclasped the collar, worried that it would stop blinking or worse. It might explode, but thankfully it did not. She made sure that the collar was close to the bathroom for them to hear that she was indeed giving Fluffy a shower. After Fluffy's shower, she left the collar on top of her bedside table before messaging Patty to see if she had any idea of the collar's origin.

Hmm, I think some nice man gave it to us for free. He had many, and I think he said he's a vet, the message read.

Man… Man…Shoot. They're moving faster than expected.

I need to give this thing to Matthew. They might be able to track down which weirdo put this thing on him. She thought to herself before sending a text to Matthew, asking him to meet her. Matthew almost immediately agreed and suggested a place to meet. For some unknown reason, she had a feeling that she should also tell her husband about her findings, so, with a quick text, she explained that she had found a listening device and was on her way to meet the detective.

Typical Ed. Never replies to my messages. She frowned even after she had driven off. Ominously, the car that was parked in front of her house was not there anymore when she peeked through her front window.

Maybe they have shifts? That's a strange thing for a stalker.

She soon found herself parked on those tall, semi-empty commercial buildings some miles from home. She didn't understand the uneasiness she felt when she left the car, perhaps because she feared that they finally noticed that Debbie had brought the listening device with her in her bag. With a gulp, she called Matthew on the phone, who instructed her to go to the fourth floor of the almost empty building. The first floor had a security guard who only looked at her for a moment before disregarding her. It was clean, though, despite being quite deserted with some furniture wrapped in plastic. Its walls were painted white, with blue lining. Debbie sighed in relief when she saw that the elevators were working, entering one and pressing the number 4.

She checked her phone again, anxious — still no reply from Ed.

Gravity

Ding!

Debbie breathed out as the elevator door opened. The floor was much more maintained and well-lit. The flooring had a hexagon-shaped designed carpet with grey tones; the walls were white, and the ceiling had a slight dug-out box-like cut running along the corridor where the florescent lights were. There weren't many doors. Debbie counted at least 5 of them that were a dark walnut color.

Matthew said he's the last door on the left- oh, there it is.

Debbie carefully rang the doorbell. A few moments later, the door revealed Matthew, who was wearing a button-up, blue-colored shirt and black slacks, his hair a little less styled than the last time they met.

"Hi. Come in. Want some drinks? Juice? Coffee? Chocolate? Tea? Oh, I think I have some red wine here as well. Let me check." Matthew said. That was the busiest and most attentive she had seen him, and she felt proud that he had admitted that he liked her.

"Water's fine." She giggled, marveling at the place. It was spacious and minimalistic, with mostly monochrome colors and silver. His couch was black leather with a white feathery throw pillow. He even had a cool modern fireplace just below his 55-inch flat screen tv that was mounted on the wall. There were also paintings, mostly abstract, and she even spotted a telescope near the window wall.

"Nice place you got here," Debbie commented as Matthew got a glass of water for her before taking a seat, a glass of wine in hand.

"It's not much, but I like it. So, what did you want to talk about?" He asked, taking a sip. Matthew clearly stiffened when Debbie leaned closer to his ear. "Debbie, what-"

"You won't believe this… but I found a listening device from Fluffy's collar. It was blinking, so I knew it was strange. There was no camera. I checked already. I have it in my bag right now."

Debbie studied his expression, catching glimpses of emotions that flashed too quickly to decipher.

"You did?"

She nodded, planting her index finger vertically on her lips to signal him to be quiet before fishing out the device. Matthew immediately grabbed the collar, checking it before throwing it on the floor and stepping on it. The cracking sound it made caused Debbie to gasp in disbelief.

"Why did you do that?! How can we find whoever put it on him?!" Debbie asked in frustration, but Matthew remained calm.

"It's fine. They must've already known that you noticed since the blinking stopped."

"Still, we could've tracked them down!"

"No, they could've tracked us faster. Or it could've exploded if I hadn't disposed of it." Matthew smiled at her softly. "You did great, though, telling me this. You should consider joining the team so we can get together more often."

All her frustration was thrown out the window as Debbie blushed at his comment. "There you go again, sweet talking your way in."

Matthew only chuckled, sweeping the broken particles away with a broom. It was endearing to watch him do that, something Ed never did. Ed never liked household chores and always told Debbie to just hire a house cleaner or go to the dry cleaner. He never enjoyed the simple things Debbie enjoyed, and when she tried to join him in whatever he was doing, he would just stop completely, saying it was nothing.

Fishing her phone out, she grimaced.

Ed had still not replied to her text.

"Penny, for your thoughts?" Debbie snapped out of her reverie when Matthew placed a handful of pennies in front of her face, smiling playfully at her. She laughed lightly, taking a penny.

"Hmm." She commented with an enthusiastic nod.

"You can have more if you'd like," he replied, chuckling, before continuing. "So, what's on your mind?"

Debbie pursed her lips, wondering if this topic would be good for someone who was basically dating her. "It's… I was thinking how Ed never really liked chores. And how he never replied to my text. It's weird, isn't it? I'm here with you, but I'm still thinking of him."

"I don't think it's weird." He spoke, soft yet determined, as he placed the remaining pennies back in their glass jar, wiping his hand with wet wipes and tossing them into the trash. "I think it's normal since you're married to him."

"Right." She muttered, her smile turning more mellow. "I'm sorry I'm telling you this…."

"It's nothing. I'm happy you can confide in me."

Debbie then gasped inwardly as Matthew kneeled in front of her, taking both her hands as he held them lovingly. She stared at those bewitching eyes, hoping to find whatever was missing inside her.

"But I must admit, Debbie. It pains me to see you settle for a man who doesn't deserve your love." The detective continued on by leaning closer and stealing a chaste kiss. "I'll do better. I'll be better for you, Debbie. Just give me a chance."

"... I... I'll think about it. Can you wait for my answer?"

Matthew smiled. "No matter how long it takes..."

Debbie smiled back before taking a deep breath. "I should go home now. Fluffy is there alone, and I'm worried."

"I understand." He said, standing up to usher Debbie towards the hallway. Matthew questioned, "Are you sure you don't want me to walk you to your car?"

Debbie shook her head no. "It's fine. It's still early, and I doubt someone followed me here."

"I see. Well, drive home safely, and remember to text me when you get back, and please don't tell your husband about the card. I don't trust him."

"... *Yeah*. Sure. I'm going now then. Fluffy might be hungry. Bye."

"Bye."

Debbie speed-walked towards the elevator, grateful that it was already there as she pressed the *ground floor*. She waited, sweating and jittery, for the door to close. And it was about to until a hand forcefully stopped it from closing fully, making Debbie scream in surprise.

"M-Matthew, what's going on?" She stammered, pupils shaking as she tried to hold her ground. Matthew's demeanor drastically changed, a brooding cloud on his face as he smiled hauntingly at her.

"You never mentioned anything about the card, did you?" He asked, his voice turning dark.

"W-what do you mean. I did mention it. Weren't you paying attention?" She tried to laugh it off. "Really, I need to go home now. Let's talk about it over the phone."

Debbie tried pressing the ground floor button repeatedly, but Matthew wouldn't move away from the elevator door. She sucked in a breath as she heard his low chuckling while he ruffled his already unruly hair.

"Ah, such a shame. I thought I would've gotten away with this a little longer."

Debbie became pale when the look in his eyes changed. *This, this must be the real Matthew, horrifying, dangerous, a far cry from the man he was with me.*

"You're scaring me." She admitted, hoping that the man had even a speck of real attraction as to let her free. But no, Matthew only grabbed her upper arm and dragged her out of the elevator with Debbie screaming bloody murder. By pure instinct and sheer adrenaline rush, Debbie did something she never thought she could.

Matthew cried out as Debbie plunged the metal rat tail comb into his hand that was gripping her arm. She scurried away towards the fire exit. The stairs going to the third floor were blocked off by a tall metal fence with a lock.

"What the- why is there a fence here?!" she cried out, panicking as she heard Matthew calling out for her to come out. With few options, she ran up to the fifth floor. Again, the door to the hallway was locked.

"Debbie! Come back here, you little-"

Debbie couldn't hear the end of it as she rushed another floor up and another until she finally found an open door. To her dismay, it was the rooftop.

"Ah, how unfortunate. You ran out of places to escape."

Debbie spun around to see that Matthew had already caught up with her. She cried, "Why are you doing this to me, Matthew? I trusted you."

"I know. You were so easy to fool. It was fun playing detective with you. However, it's unfortunate that you found out so soon. It would've been priceless if we had gotten married and you'd found out who I really was. Though that dog must go if that happened, he tried biting me. Funny how your dog has a better survival instinct than you."

"So, it's all a lie? What you said? What you feel? You said I could trust you."

Matthew shrugged. "I did say you could trust me. But I never said I would never lie."

Debbie questioned, "What are you? Who are you really?"

"Who I am matters little to this conversation. But I'll tell you." Matthew moved even closer, and that's when Debbie realized she had reached a dead end as the warm railings prevented her from falling to her death. Memories of Philip threatening her flashed before her eyes as she started panting.

Matthew grabbed both her shoulders with a menacing smirk and whispered, "I'm a spy."

Debbie screamed as Matthew pushed her off the railings, albeit reacting fast enough to grab him with one hand while the other gripped the railing for dear life.

"You jerk!" Matthew shouted angrily as he clasped her hand, falling over the railing. Debbie held on tightly, feeling like both her arms were being ripped off, the burning sensation crawling under her skin.

Ah. I haven't solved the case… but I don't think I can ever survive this. She thought to herself as tears rolled down her face. How unlucky she was to have met such an attractive man, only for him to end up being her worst nightmare.

Nightmare, perhaps ending this nightmare here would be better. Ed… I'm sorry.

Debbie closed her eyes and prepared to let go of the railings when two warm hands grabbed the hand she had on the railing.

"Debbie! Hang on!"

Fluttering her eyes open, she choked a sob as she saw her husband struggling to pull her to safety.

"Let go of him, Debbie! You have to!" Ed shouted. Looking down, she noted the fear in Matthew's eyes. Those were the eyes she'd almost fallen in love with.

"Please, Debbie. I meant nothing I said. I-I... I was only asked to do so. I really like you. I love you, Debbie. Please don't let go," he pleaded.

Ed shouted, "Don't listen to him! He's brainwashing you! Come on, let go of that bastard!"

Matthew pleaded, "Please… *you love me, right?*"

Debbie clenched her fist before looking at Matthew.

Debbie let go and watched as he fell to his death, her heartbeat the only sound she could hear as Ed pulled her back to the rooftop. She was surprised when Ed suddenly hugged her, almost crushing her.

"I almost lost you. Thank goodness you're safe."

That's when the waterworks completely broke. Debbie clutched her clothes as she bawled her eyes out. It lasted for a while until Debbie felt well enough to walk to her car. Ed did offer to carry her, but she declined. She was still shaken up that the entire ride home was quicker than getting to the building.

"We're here," Ed announced as Debbie nodded and thanked him. She walked, almost losing balance, in a daze, but thankfully Ed was fast enough to catch her.

It doesn't make sense. Matthew was supposed to be a good guy. He was supposed to be the guy that would change her perspective on love. She was supposed to love him, and he was supposed to love her.

"You did the right thing, Debbie. It wasn't your fault." Ed assured, and she knew that. She knew, and yet, it still bothered her.

"Call me if you need anything. I can't reply to your messages, but I read them. Always."

"Okay…"

"Okay… Go inside now. I'll get going too."

"Yeah. Thanks… bye."

As soon as Debbie closed the door, she fell to her knees and cried, alerting Fluffy, who came running, but Debbie stopped him.

"Don't come near me, please! I'm a murderer, Fluffy. I murdered him." She cried while the dog whimpered in response.

"I killed him. I killed Matthew. I'm no different."

Judy's killer, Herman's, what difference does it make when Debbie had soiled her hands with blood now?

None. The answer was none. *I am a murderer now, too.*

Did you enjoy this book?

Ready for more? Follow this and other favorites below!

https://www.ttpublishinghouse.com/legendsreborn

https://www.ttpublishinghouse.com/7wishes

https://www.ttpublishinghouse.com/mallcadet